Rudy Toot-Toot

by
Rick Daley

Rudy Toot-Toot

Copyright © 2012 by Richard J. Daley

This book is a work of fiction. Any resemblances to any person, living or dead, events, or locales, is entirely coincidental.

ISBN: 1468168533
ISBN-13: 978-1468168532

Interior book design by Rick Daley
Illustrations by Colleen Comer
Cover design by CreateSpace

DEDICATION

To everyone who has ever tried and failed:
May you find the courage to try again.

And, of course, to my wife and kids, because
they are awesome.

Chapter 1

Over the river and halfway to the middle of nowhere stood a bean farm, and on that farm there lived a young boy named Rudy Toot-Toot. Rudy was no ordinary boy, mind you. He had a special power, almost like a superhero.

What was his special power, you ask?

Rudy Toot-Toot could fart.

Sometimes they were harmless little toots:

Pfft.

Other times they were regular old farts:

Pfffffffffffffffffffft!

But once in a while, Rudy would let out a Big One—a fart so loud it made a shotgun blast sound like a firecracker and so strong it made a hurricane feel like a summer breeze:

PFFFFFFFFFFFFFFFFFFFFFFFFFFFFFFT!

Now before you tell me there's nothing special about farting—and you'd be right, for the most part—let me tell you a story about Rudy Toot-Toot and you might change your mind.

Let's be clear, though: Rudy's farts weren't always special. They actually got him into a lot of trouble at first.

Even his regular farts had enough wind power to blow over a tractor (it happened at least once a year). He could even make it sound—and smell—like his farts came from someone else; he called that his *ventrilo-gas* trick. And even though he could fart on command, every time (except once...more on that later), the problem was that Rudy couldn't hold his farts in when he was supposed to, or control the power of a Big One.

Rudy thought his farts were really funny. Everyone else thought his farts were really rude. Mama Toot-Toot called Rudy "courtesy-challenged."

Rudy had a good heart and he meant well, but as Papa Toot-Toot put it, Rudy never thought about "the consequences of his actions."

Papa used big words like *consequences* a lot, and poor Rudy never had the faintest idea what Papa was talking about.

Papa also said, "There's a time and a place for everything." Then he would usually say, "And this was neither the right time nor the right place..." He could go on for hours about self-control, and common courtesy, and respect for your peers, and blah blah blah blah blah.

It didn't matter. Papa's lectures could not stop Rudy from farting. You see, Rudy ate beans for breakfast, lunch, and dinner. He loved them: pinto beans, fava beans, lima beans, garbanzo beans, kidney beans, green beans...even peanuts (because they're really beans, too). And eating all those beans...well, *that* had consequences.

It's a well-known fact that beans make you fart. There's even an old rhyme about it:

> *Beans, beans, the magical fruit,*
> *The more you eat, the more you toot.*
> *The more you toot, the better you feel,*
> *So have some beans at every meal!*

Rudy loved that rhyme. He liked the idea that his farts were magic. That's why, instead of saying "Excuse me" when he farted, Rudy said "Abracadabra!"—when he remembered to say anything at all.

Rudy's lack of self-control frustrated Mama and Papa. Even more frustrated was Rudy's big sister, Judy, who *never* farted. But that's okay. Rudy farted enough for both of them (and then some).

But the members of Rudy's family weren't the only ones affected by his affliction. Everyone—from Rudy's schoolmates to the hired hands who helped manage the farm to the Beanheads who camped along the road during the harvest season waiting to buy their favorite beans—everyone had suffered from at least one of Rudy's slip-ups. Rudy was left out, laughed at, and—to many—a lost cause.

One year, though, that all changed.

CHapter 2

Springtime. The sun rises earlier and sets later. The cold days of winter melt into memories as the ground thaws, getting ready for another growing season. Living on a farm, Rudy Toot-Toot learned to watch the changing of the seasons—they told him how hard he had to work.

When fall turned to winter, there were no plants to grow or harvest. That's when he didn't work at all. Rudy loved the winter. It was full of snowball fights and sledding.

When winter turned to spring, he helped get the fields ready by tilling them, pulling heavy ploughs behind tractors. Rudy liked tilling the fields. That part was fun, because he got to ride on the tractor and it did all the work.

Once the fields were tilled, Rudy helped sow the seeds, spreading and planting them over hundreds of acres of farmland. That part was a lot harder, but it was worth it because he got an extra week off from school.

Rudy pulled weeds all through summer vacation. It almost made him wish he was back in school.

Almost.

When summer came to an end and school started again, it was time for the harvest. Beans had to be picked, sorted, bagged, tagged, and sold at the Toot-Toot Family Bean Market. That's when everyone worked the hardest.

~∞~

One spring morning, Rudy's early-bird alarm went off inside him and his eyes popped open. It was very early, but since he didn't have school that day, Rudy crawled out of bed. (Rudy always snoozed through his early-bird alarm and stayed in bed on school days.)

He walked over to the window and looked out at the freshly tilled fields. The orange tip of the sun was just peeking over the horizon, and its light made the morning dew twinkle like fields of diamonds.

Rudy watched their old rooster strut out of the barn and over to the fencepost. It eyed the top of the post with the confidence of a lion getting ready to pounce on a mouse. The rooster scratched the ground, clucked twice, and jumped with all its might. It missed. Rudy heard the *thonk* all the way in his bedroom as the rooster knocked its head into the bottom rail of the fence.

The stubborn old bird did not give up. It took a step back, adjusted its aim, and jumped again, this time sailing over the fence and into the bushes on the other side. The rooster untangled itself from the branches and tried one more time. It finally made it, clutching the top of the fencepost with its feet, its wings flapping wildly to stay balanced.

Rudy kept an eye on the rooster. He wanted to get his timing just right. It was an important day: The first day of the planting season. Everyone had to get up early and get started. Rudy would make sure that happened. The rooster cocked his head back to let out a loud "cock-a-doodle-do" so he could wake everyone up, but as he did...

Pfffffffffffffffffffffffffffffffffffffffffffffffft!

Rudy beat him to it.

"Abracadabra," Rudy said as his fart echoed through the hallways of the house. It rattled the plumbing, making pings and tings chase each other through the walls. The ground outside trembled. The rooster jumped off the fence post and ran back to the barn as the dew drops all exploded from the force of the blast, leaving a fine mist in their wake.

"Good morning, Rudy," Mama and Papa called from their bedroom.

"Rudy Toot-Toot, how rude!" Judy yelled from her room.

Rudy got dressed and went downstairs to watch television. He flipped past all the shows with boring adults talking until he found a cartoon. Judy came down and tried to wrestle the remote control away from him so she could watch the beauty tips on one of the morning shows. Mama came down and headed right to the kitchen to make the family her special 5-bean omelets for breakfast.

Rudy and Judy stood in the middle of the family room, the remote control between them like the rope in a game of tug-o-war.

"Give it back!" Rudy said and pulled on the remote. "I was here first."

"You got to pick the show yesterday. Besides, you've seen this before," Judy said as the cartoon cut to a commercial.

"Fine then," Rudy said and let go of the remote, sending Judy flailing backward. She tripped over the coffee table and tumbled onto the couch. Rudy thought about apologizing, but he was laughing too hard and couldn't catch his breath.

Judy sat up and changed the channel, satisfied that she had won the battle. She ran her fingers through her hair to straighten it, then smoothed out her shirt so she wouldn't look frumpy at school.

"Your omelets are ready," Mama called. Rudy hurried to the kitchen for his favorite breakfast, Judy followed close behind him.

Rudy lifted a cold glass of milk to his lips and was mid-gulp when Papa walked into the kitchen with his shirt on backwards and his underwear on the outside of his pants. Rudy laughed so hard milk shot out of his nose like sea mist exploding from the blowhole of a whale. The spray landed right on Judy's face.

"Rudy Toot-Toot, how rude!" Judy yelled as she reached for a napkin to wipe herself off.

Papa seemed not to notice. He just sat down on his regular chair at the table. Mama poured him a cup of coffee and set an omelet down in front of him. Rudy watched Papa put a huge scoop of salt in his coffee and sprinkle sugar all over his eggs.

Papa took a sip of coffee. The salt made him gag and spit. Hot coffee erupted from his mouth like lava from a volcano...drenching poor Judy for a second time! She screamed and ran upstairs to the bathroom. When Rudy heard the shower come on he knew that nobody would see Judy again for at least an hour, and the house wouldn't have hot water again until the next day.

"What's wrong, dear?" Mama asked Papa.

"First planting day of the season," Papa said.

"I don't know why you always get so worked up. You've been doing this your whole life, and every year you start the first planting day with your undies in a knot."

"No knots today!" Papa said and pointed to his underpants. "I'm not taking any chances. I'm doing everything the lucky way today."

Mama rolled her eyes and gave Papa The Look. The Look could mean many different things. For Judy, The Look typically meant that Mama was proud of a straight-A report card. For Rudy, The Look usually meant that he farted in the wrong place or the wrong time again. This time, for Papa, The Look definitely meant he could not go to work wearing his underwear on the outside of his pants.

"I'll go upstairs and change," Papa said and excused himself from the table.

Later, when Papa came back down dressed the right way, Rudy asked him why he worried so much on the first planting day.

"Well, Rudy," Papa said, "let me explain it to you..." and Rudy immediately regretted asking him. Papa talked. And talked. And talked. And talked. He explained, in painful detail, every little thing that worried him. Since the first planting day was the beginning of the whole growing season, all his worries for the entire year stemmed from it. Weeds, bugs, money, the bank, something called a lien...Papa kept talking until Judy was out of the shower *and* her hair was dry. The more he talked, the less Rudy understood.

Then Papa said something that made sense: "No more pizza."

There was only one thing in the world Rudy liked to eat better than beans: Pizza! Pizza was a special treat because no one delivered out to the farm. They had to go to Emilio's in town for pizza, and it took almost an hour to get there so they hardly ever got to go. Papa was finally speaking Rudy's language, and now Rudy was worried, too.

"How can I help?" Rudy asked. "I'll do whatever it takes!"

"You can help plant the soybeans today. They're our number-one cash crop."

Cash crop? Rudy pictured a plant with a bunch of dollar bills instead of leaves, and bean pods filled with quarters, nickels, and dimes. "I thought you said money doesn't grow on trees. But it grows on beans?"

"For us it does! Rudy, the cash comes from people who buy the beans, not from the plants," Papa explained.

"What about our corn?" Rudy asked. "Is that a cash crop, too?"

"No, the corn is for Mr. Anderson. We grow it for him, and he uses it to feed his cows."

"So he gets the corn for free?" Rudy asked. "I'd rather have money so we can buy pizza!"

"We trade. He gives us milk, meat, and free ice cream."

Rudy liked Mr. Anderson's ice cream, especially the vanilla, made fresh with Toot-Toot vanilla beans.

"When do we start planting?" Rudy asked.

"Go get Mama and Judy and meet me in the barn in fifteen minutes," Papa said.

CHAPTER 3

Rudy, Judy, and Mama went out to the barn and met Papa and Big Bean Dean, the head of the hired hands. Big Bean Dean was so tall that when he stood up outside, he bumped his head on birds. Wearing his green work shirt Big Bean Dean looked like a giant string bean.

"Dean, is the crew ready to go?" Papa asked.

"I'm ready to go," Rudy said, and he let loose with a blast of gas.

Pfffffffffffffffffffffffffft!

It was just a normal toot, by Rudy's standards, but it still blew the doors off the barn. "Abracadabra!" he said, laughing.

"Rudy Toot-Toot, how rude! Your farts aren't magic, they're just gross. Why can't you say 'excuse me' like a normal person? Or better yet, not fart at all?" Judy asked. She *never* thought Rudy's farts were funny.

"Rudy, there's a time and a place for everything..." Papa started.

"And now it's time to plant the beans, and the place is the soybean field," Big Bean Dean said. He had to stop Papa. If he started in on a lecture, they wouldn't have time left to plant anything that day.

"Right. We're going to work together and plant the soybeans one-by-one," Papa said. "By hand."

Rudy and Judy both groaned. They would have rather used machines to help with the planting. Doing it by hand sounded like too much work! But Papa said they would be planting soybeans by hand. And Papa never changed his mind about stuff like that. So planting soybeans by hand it was.

The hired hands loaded up a big cart and hitched it to the tractor. It was too full for Rudy to ride on, so he walked next to Judy as they left for the soybean field. They had to cross several fields to get there. As they walked, Rudy overheard Papa explain to the hired hands how the soybean field was the very best field on the farm, and since his soybeans were his most important cash crop they absolutely, positively had to grow there.

Rudy felt a rumbling in his tummy. "Wanna pull my finger?" he asked Judy.

"Gosh, let me think about it...*NO!* I know better than that, Rudy. You're just going to fart. You always fart. And I don't want to be near you when you do it," Judy said and started walking faster.

Next to her is always the wrong place, Rudy thought.

Rudy walked over to Big Bean Dean. "Hi Dean," he said.

"No, Rudy. I don't want to pull your finger," Dean said, and patted him on the head instead.

How did he know? Rudy thought. He really wished someone would pull his finger, then he could let loose with the 5-bean fart that had been building up since breakfast.

They finally got to the soybean field. It was right next to the field where they grew Mr. Anderson's corn last year. Rudy watched as the hired hands unloaded all the seeds, mounding them up in piles as tall as Big Bean Dean all along one edge of the field. They made one pile for each row to be planted.

Mama wanted them to sing to the seeds while they planted. She said it helped the seeds to know they were loved, which made them grow better. Rudy thought it made him look silly. But he knew that when Mama got an idea in her head, it was best to just go along with it. When Mama was happy, the whole family was happy.

"Here's what you need to do," Papa said. "Take a soybean seed, and push it down into the ground. It needs to be an inch-and-a-half deep. Then cover it loosely with soil. This should be easy, but we have a big field so it will take a while."

"And don't forget to sing," Judy reminded everyone. Mama smiled. Rudy groaned.

CHAPTER 4

Rudy walked over to the cart behind the tractor and picked out a belt with a pouch attached to it. He liked to fasten the belt loose so the pouch would hang low on his hip. It made him feel like a gunslinger in one of the cowboy movies Papa liked to watch.

Before he could put the belt on, he saw something moving on the ground. At first he thought it was a small snake, but it was actually a really big worm. It was the biggest worm Rudy had ever seen!

When a boy sees something as spectacular as a gigantic earthworm, there's only one thing he can do: catch it. There was more to it than just the thrill of the hunt, though. Rudy knew that worms meant good, healthy soil. He wanted to catch the worm so he could show Papa. Maybe if Papa saw the worm he would stop being so worried about planting day. He would know that the soil was good and his cash crop would make him rich.

Rudy tried to grab the worm, but it squirmed under a big clod of soil. Rudy picked the clod up and saw the worm slide into a deep crack, trying to burrow into the moist ground. Rudy tossed the hunk of dirt aside, his excitement building inside him. But that was not all that was building inside him. The extra helping of 5-bean omelet churned in his belly, and pressure began to build.

The worm was about to get away, but Rudy dug after it. That was when he bent over.

When he was standing up Rudy could hold his farts in for a little while, but when he bent over he could never hold his farts in, and the one inside him was a Big One. The Biggest One so far that year.

Rudy dug for the worm, his butt pointed at the piles of soybean seeds. The gas rumbled through his belly, racing toward freedom. Rudy finally grabbed the worm and shouted, "Papa, look at..."

PFFFFFFFFFFFFFFFFFFFFFFFFFFFFFFFT!

Nobody heard his shout. All they heard was the thunderous roar of his fart. Its wind hit the piles of seeds with hurricane force, blasting each pile and sending all the seeds soaring. The ground trembled under their feet and birds struggled to stay in the air.

"Abracadabra!" Rudy said, watching the seeds rise high into the air.

"Rudy Toot-Toot, how rude!" Mama said. "That's not the kind of music the seeds needed to hear..."

The plunking sound of falling beans caught everyone's attention. Even Mama stopped her scolding, and they all watched as the seeds rained down—all over the wrong field. It began as a light pattering but quickly grew to a downpour.

The seeds came down in the field where they grew Mr. Anderson's corn last year, not in the soybean field Papa had so carefully prepared. They rained down in neat little rows, one for each pile. They flew so high that when they hit the ground they dug down into the soil. The trembling earth shifted the dirt, covering up the holes where the beans lay.

Papa and Big Bean Dean raced over to the cornfield, trying to mark the places where the soybeans fell.

"Do you think we can dig them up and re-plant them?" Big Bean Dean asked Papa.

Papa shook his head. "By the time we find them all, it will be too late to re-plant them today. Besides, it's supposed to rain hard tonight and then clear up for the rest of the week. This is the ideal time to get them in the ground. We'll just have to let them grow here and hope for the best."

"We can still sing to them," Mama said. "In fact, it's more important now than ever before."

No one could think of a good reason to disagree with Mama, so the whole Toot-Toot family joined the hired hands and spread out across the vast field.

"Rudy, I want you to sing the loudest, because you are the one who got us into this mess!" Mama said, and she started to sing:

> *Our seeds grow best with love and care*
> *So you know what that means*
> *You sing with me and then we'll see*
> *The world's best tootin' beans*

Rudy sang the best he could, even though he felt silly doing it. He felt really bad about blowing the beans into the wrong field.

Later that evening, after dinner, Papa called Rudy out to sit with him on the front porch. Rudy walked slowly and stopped at the door. He reached up and grabbed the handle but he didn't turn it. Rudy just stood there, dreading the lecture that surely awaited him.

Papa must have heard him because he said, "Come on out, Rudy."

Rudy opened the door and stepped down onto the porch. Papa was sitting in his rocking chair. Rudy walked over to the porch swing and sat down next to him.

"Rudy, I know you have a special gift," Papa said. "You can fart better than anyone in the world. I'm sure of it. But there is a time and a place for everything and today was simply the wrong time and the wrong place. You missed by a mile today, son. You may have ruined the crop. You have got to try harder to control yourself."

"Yessir," Rudy said. He looked Papa in the eyes. He could tell that Papa was not mad at him. He was just worried about the beans—more worried than ever before.

Papa stood up and Rudy did, too. Papa put his hand on Rudy's shoulder as they walked inside.

"Someday, son, I know you'll find out how to use your amazing gift. But not today. You need to get cleaned up and get to bed. You go back to school tomorrow."

"Goodnight, Papa," Rudy said as he climbed up the stairs.

"Goodnight, Rudy."

CHAPTER 5

Rudy didn't mind school, for the most part. Fourth grade wasn't much harder than third grade, and he had plenty of friends to play with at recess. He hated getting out of bed in the morning, though. Rudy usually did anything he could think of to stay under the covers a little bit longer. Sometimes he would pull the sheets over his head and pretend he was sound asleep, and that he couldn't hear Mama call him or feel her poke him.

But some days—like the day he was supposed to read a book report in front of the entire class, a book report that was assigned on Monday, due on Friday, and somehow forgotten about until Thursday—those days called for more drastic measures.

"I don't feel good," Rudy told Mama as she pulled back the covers on his bed. He hid his head under the pillow.

"What's the matter today?" Mama asked, sounding doubtful.

"My stomach hurts."

Mama put her hand on Rudy's forehead. "Ninety-eight point six. You don't have a fever."

"How do you know? You didn't even use the thermometer!"

Mama went to the hall closet and got the digital thermometer. "Open," she said.

Rudy opened his mouth and she slid the tip of the thermometer under his tongue. He closed his mouth and tried his best to feel warm. He thought about fire and volcanoes.

After a minute the thermometer beeped. Mama pulled it out of his mouth and looked at the screen. She showed it to Rudy. Ninety-eight point six, exactly. *How does she do that?*

"You probably just have gas. Go to the bathroom and do your thing. And try not to blow all the water out of the toilet bowl this time."

"I know," Rudy said.

"Then hurry up and get dressed and brush your teeth. You can't miss the bus. Papa and I can't drive you to school today. We have more planting to do."

"Can't I just stay home?"

"No," Mama said, and that was that. She really knew how to get to the point sometimes.

Rudy got dressed and went to the bathroom to brush his teeth. His shaggy mop of red hair stuck up in all directions, and even though he wet his comb, his hair refused to lie down. Rudy scrunched his freckled cheeks.

Great. Now I'll have to stand in front of the class looking like a goofball!

Rudy ate breakfast—a bacon, egg, and bean burrito—and went out front with Judy to wait for the bus.

When he got to school, Rudy trudged to his classroom. His teacher wasn't there yet. He hoped for a substitute, one that wouldn't know about the book reports. He was pretty sure Mrs. Miller said it had to be a chapter book, but there was no way he could read an entire chapter book *and* write a two-page book report in one night.

Rudy had picked the shortest book he could find on the bookshelf in his bedroom, a picture book. It would have to do.

A swarm of butterflies fluttered through his stomach when Mrs. Miller walked into the room. Mrs. Miller had been Papa's teacher when he was a boy. The older kids said she taught Abe Lincoln *and* George Washington, and she was old back then. Despite her age, Mrs. Miller commanded more authority than a lion tamer. And she didn't even need to use a whip.

"Today you will each read your book report out loud in front of the class," Mrs. Miller said as the students took their seats. Her voice sounded like the pencil sharpener when it got stuck.

The dreaded moment was at hand. Hopefully Mrs. Miller would call the class alphabetically by last name, and Davy Anderson would have to go first. Or by first name, and Aaron Rogers would be up. Either way, Rudy Toot-Toot was going to be near the end of the list, and he hoped they would run out of time before they got to him. And since it was Friday, that meant he would be safe until Monday.

"We'll go alphabetically by first name..."

Awesome! Sorry about your luck, Aaron.

"...but we'll go backwards. Zachary is out sick today..."

His Mama must not be able to take his temperature with her hand.

"...so that means Rudy will get to go first. Come on up, Rudy."

Dang! Rudy got up and walked to the front of the classroom holding his book report in his hands. His tummy rumbled. He felt a fart coming on.

Rudy stood at the front of the room facing the class and began to read his report. "My book was *The Little Engine That Could...*"

Pfffft! Rudy farted. Not a Big One, but it was loud enough to echo down the hallway. The whole class started giggling, and Rudy heard the kids in the class across the hall giggle, too.

"Kids, calm down. Rudy, please continue," Mrs. Miller said, sitting at her desk.

"It's about a train that tries to..."

Pfffffffffffffft! Rudy farted again, longer this time and just as loud.

More giggles. Rudy continued, "I mean, the train has trouble going..."

Pfffffffffffffffffffffffffffffffffffffffffffffffffft!

This one lasted for almost a minute, and it was loud enough to rattle the chalkboard and turn the chalk in the tray into dust.

Open laughter shook the room. Aaron Rogers laughed so hard he fell out of his chair. Mrs. Miller stood up and walked to the front of the room.

"Rudy, you need to stop expelling gas. It's getting very disruptive," she said. "Class, flatulence is a natural bodily function. It is not funny."

That may have been true for most adults, but not for most kids. For most kids, farts were funny. *Very* funny. In fact, the only kid Rudy knew who didn't think farts were funny was his sister Judy. But she didn't think *anything* was funny, so she didn't count.

"The train keeps saying I think I..."

Pffft!

"I think I..."

Pffft!

"I think I..."

Pffft!

Rudy was belting them out on purpose now, trying his hardest to make his friends laugh.

Rudy relished every last chuckle. Unfortunately for him, Mrs. Miller did not.

"Rudy Toot-Toot, that's enough! Accidental flatulence is one thing, but now you are just exacerbating the situation."

Exacerbating the situation? So she's the one who taught Papa to talk like that...

"Class, I want you to read quietly until I get back. Rudy, come with me." Mrs. Miller started toward the door. She led Rudy straight to the principal's office.

Mr. Antwon, the principal, sat at his desk and tried not to laugh as Mrs. Miller explained how Rudy turned her carefully structured learning environment into a laughing-gas chamber. Mr. Antwon feared Mrs. Miller as much as the students did (she had once been his teacher, too) so he didn't argue when she suggested a one-hour detention for Rudy after school.

Rudy gasped. A detention meant he would miss the bus. And that meant that Mama would have to come pick him up. And *that* meant Rudy was going to be in big trouble when he got home.

At lunchtime Judy walked over to Rudy in the cafeteria. "I hear you have a detention and you have to stay late. You're going to be in so much trouble! I don't want to be there when Mama picks you up," she said, and then she did something totally out of character. She actually laughed.

Judy's giggles burned in Rudy's ears as she walked away. He didn't want to be there when Mama picked him up, either.

Surprisingly, Mama didn't scold him when she picked him up. In fact, neither she nor Papa said a single word to Rudy all night.

~∞~

The next morning Rudy watched Papa drink his coffee on the front porch. A broad smile crossed Papa's face as he admired the green field of soybean sprouts. *Maybe they weren't so mad about yesterday,* Rudy thought.

"Will the beans grow good, Papa?" Rudy asked as he sat down on the swing next to him.

"I think so. They look very strong. They must be very good seeds," Papa said.

"We better get to planting the rest of the fields," Rudy said.

"Rudy, you go play in the yard. We'll be able to sow the rest of the seeds without you," Papa said.

Rudy frowned. "But I want to help!"

"Your time will come. But after your performance in the soybean field, and your outbursts at school yesterday, it's become apparent that you can't control yourself. We can't risk any further incidents," Papa said. Rudy didn't know exactly what *risk further incidents* meant, other than *no*.

Rudy stuffed his hands into his pockets and walked back to the yard. He passed Judy, who was heading out to the fields.

"I get to plant the peanuts," Judy said with a smirk.

Rudy let out two little toots that sounded a lot like the words *big deal*.

"Rudy Toot-Toot, how rude!" Judy turned her nose up and hurried off to the peanut field.

Rudy climbed up the ladder to the fort atop his swing-set and looked through the telescope mounted to the wall. He scanned the fields.

Rudy could see everything on the farm from up there. The hired hands were hard at work, sowing seeds. Papa and Big Bean Dean were planting corn where the soybeans were supposed to be. He saw Judy way off in the distance, planting peanuts.

Rudy zeroed in on the soybeans. They were all above ground and growing taller each day. He felt bad about blasting the seeds into the cornfield, but it was an accident, and the crop wasn't ruined. He was mad at Papa for not letting him help.

Sometimes grown-ups can be so unfair, he thought. *I'll show them. One day, I'll fart and it will be the right place and the right time, and they'll be begging me to do it again!*

CHapter 6

The last day of school that year started as normally as any other day, but it sure ended differently. In the morning, Rudy sat next to Judy on the bus, like always. Judy complained when Rudy farted, as usual. Rudy farted whenever the bus went over the tiniest bump, without fail. And the road was so dimpled and bumpy you'd think it was paved with Legos and golf balls.

Mr. Antwon, the principal, stood outside the school greeting the kids as they got off the bus. When Rudy walked past him Mr. Antwon said, "Rudy Toot-Toot, I need to talk to you."

And that's when the day stopped being normal.

"Now?" Rudy asked. *What could he want to talk to me about? Am I in trouble again? I have to think fast and get out of this.*

"Sure. Why not?" Mr. Antwon asked.

"I really have to go to the bathroom." *Good one!*

"Okay, but come to my office before the bell rings."

"Yessir." *Dang!*

Rudy scurried off to the bathroom and went into one of the stalls. He closed and locked the door and stood leaning against the wall.

What could Mr. Antwon want to talk to me about? I didn't do anything he doesn't already know about, did I? I can't get a detention on the last day of school!

Rudy didn't move. Several minutes passed. He was about to leave when someone came into the bathroom. Hard-soled shoes clacked on the tile floor. Rudy knew that sound.

Mr. Antwon! Rudy stood on the toilet seat so Mr. Antwon wouldn't see his feet if he looked under the stall door.

Rudy concentrated. He knew how to get out of this. *Right place, right time...*Rudy thought, and he produced a special fart. A *ventrilo-gas* fart. Rudy threw the sound and it landed in the stall farthest from him: **Pffft.**

Mr. Antwon turned toward the far stall. He walked over to it and stood outside the door. Rudy opened the door to his stall and peeked out.

"Rudy, is that you?" Mr. Antwon said, knocking on the door of the far stall. He had his back to Rudy, who quickly slipped out of the bathroom and ran to his classroom.

Rudy hung up his backpack and took his seat. Mr. Antwon came on the loudspeaker and started his morning announcements.

Mr. Antwon is back in his office, he stopped looking for me! "Woot, woot!" Rudy shouted.

"Rudy Toot-Toot, how rude! You know better than to disrupt the morning announcements. Another outburst and I'll send you to the principal's office," said Mrs. Miller. The rest of the class giggled.

"Sorry, ma'am. I'm just, er...looking forward to summer vacation," Rudy stammered. "I'll be quiet."

The last day of school was only a half-day. The class didn't have any work to do, so they played games in the classroom until recess. After recess, the whole school would attend the end-of-year ceremony out in the stadium. After the ceremony, the busses would take all the kids home. All Rudy needed to do was make it to the bus without running into Mr. Antwon again and he would be safe until September.

The bell rang and it was time for recess. Rudy poked his head into the hallway and looked to his left. The coast was clear. He looked to the right. The coast was clear...and then Mr. Antwon turned the corner!

Rudy bolted from the room and ran down the hall in the other direction, escaping out the door and onto the busy playground. He ran past the swings to the big tractor tire.

The tire stood like a giant rubber arch, half of it buried in the ground. Several kids climbed its thick treads and sat on top of it. The hollow inside of the tire was big enough for two people to hide in each side. When Rudy looked inside the tire he found four kids already in there!

"Let me in, I need to hide!" Rudy said.

"No way, we were here first."

"Look, this is an emergency. One of you can go, or all of you can go," Rudy said.

"We don't have to do what you say, Rudy Toot-Toot," one boy said.

Rudy closed his eyes. He started to fart. A long, slow fart.

Pfffffffffffffffffffffffffffffffffffffffffffffffffffffffff...

"Gross!" one of the kids said.

...**fffffffffffffffffffffffffffffffffffffffffffffffffffffffff**...

"Cut it out!" yelled another.

...**fffffffffffffffffffffffffffffffffffffffffffffffffffffffff**...

Rudy turned and pointed his butt toward each side of the tire, gassing both sides equally. "Let's get out of here!" The kids all fled the toxic tire.

...**ffffffffffffffffffffft**.

Rudy smiled as he nestled into the open hollow of the tire. *Mission accomplished!*

Rudy stayed in the tire until the bell rang. Time to go inside, grab his book-bag and lunchbox, and then head out to the stadium. He stepped out of the tire and squinted in the sunlight. He expected to see Mr. Antwon standing by the door to the school, waiting for him. The door was open, but no Mr. Antwon.

Sweet! Rudy ran toward the door.

"Rudy! There you are, I've been looking for you," Mr. Antwon said, standing on top of the tire with his hand above his eyes to block the sun.

Rudy stopped dead in his tracks. *Dang!*

"Oh, yeah," Rudy said. "You wanted to talk to me. I forgot."

"That's okay. Rudy, we need your help," Mr. Antwon said, climbing down from the tire. "We have our year-end ceremony out in the stadium in a few minutes. It's too far from the school for everyone to hear the bell. I was wondering if you could give a loud toot for us to end the school year."

Rudy took a step back. *Someone is actually asking me to fart? A grown-up, no less!*

"So I'm not in trouble?" Rudy asked.

"No, Rudy. Not at all. We really need your help."

"And I won't get a detention for farting?" Rudy was still skeptical.

"No detentions, I promise." Mr. Antwon crossed his heart with his index finger.

"Well...Sure!" Rudy said. "What do you need me to do?"

"Get your things and meet me on the platform in the middle of the football field," Mr. Antwon told him.

Rudy hurried off. *This is the greatest day of my whole life!* He ran to his classroom and put on his book-bag and grabbed his lunchbox. He bumped into Judy in the hallway.

"Rudy, I saw Mr. Antwon talking to you. Do I need to tell Mama to come pick you up because you have detention again? You are going to be in *sooo* much trouble!" Judy said.

"Nope. Mr. Antwon needs my help. I'm not in any trouble at all," Rudy said, holding his chin high.

"Humph." Judy said. "We'll see." She turned and walked away.

Rudy rushed out to the football field. *This is going to be so cool!*

Mr. Antwon was there waiting. "Are you ready, Rudy?" he asked.

"I sure am!" Rudy said, and he let it rip. A Big One. It could have been his loudest fart ever. It cracked the wood on the first three rows of bleachers.

PFFFFFFFFFFFFFFFFFFFFFFFFFFFFFFT!

"No, not now! After my speech! Nobody is out here yet, Rudy. Can you do it again when I give you the signal?" Mr. Antwon said.

"I'll try," Rudy said. *Right place, wrong time. Dang!*

The students filed into the bleachers and sat down, leaving the first three rows empty for fear of splinters. The teachers joined Mr. Antwon and Rudy on the platform and Mr. Antwon gave his speech. At the end he turned to Rudy. *Now*, he mouthed and gave Rudy a thumbs-up.

Rudy tried to fart but nothing happened. He panicked. He pushed harder and a stinky little toot slipped out, but in his rush Rudy farted *ventrilo-gas* style and it landed right next to Mrs. Miller.

Pfft.

Mr. Antwon and the teachers looked at her accusingly. Mrs. Miller's wrinkled old skin turned redder than Rudy's hair, so she looked like a raisin made from a tomato.

The fart wasn't loud enough for the kids in the bleachers to hear, so Rudy tried again. He breathed deep and bent over.

A short, choppy puff of gas puttered out—the kind of fart that made Rudy want to check his underpants for skid marks—and it too failed to produce enough noise to grab the crowd's attention.

"Anytime, Rudy," Mr. Antwon said.

Rudy held his finger up. Rudy wanted Mr. Antwon to pull it, but he thought Rudy meant "give me a second" so he did nothing. Rudy pulled his own finger, a trick that never failed to produce a massive fart. Until now.

Rudy pulled each finger one at a time, and then all the fingers together on each hand. No dice. Or rather, no gas. The cheese went un-cut. For the first time in his life, Rudy was on empty. He had expelled everything on the last one, and would have to bean-up before he could fart again.

Rudy looked at Mr. Antwon. "I can't do it."

"What?" Mr. Antwon couldn't believe it.

"I'm empty." Rudy couldn't believe it, either. It was the first time in his life he couldn't fart, and hundreds of people were there waiting for him to do it! It was going to be his proudest moment.

Rudy concentrated and flexed his stomach and grunted but nothing happened.

The crowd was getting antsy. Hundreds of kids shuffled in their seats, eager to start their summer vacations. He had to fart. His school needed him. His moment in the spotlight had arrived, the defining moment in his life to date, and he was not going to blow it...and oddly enough, that was the problem.

Frustrated to the point of despair, Rudy did the only thing he could think of. He walked to the microphone, opened his mouth wide against the inside of his elbow, and blew as hard as he could. It was a trick he had witnessed many times on the playground, and for other kids it produced loud nasty fart sounds without fail. But the other kids must have practiced alone in the bathroom to perfect their tone. Rudy never did that. When you're constantly getting in trouble because you can't stop farting for real, the last thing you need to do is to learn how to fake-fart.

Rudy's attempt at a fake-fart resulted in a choppy squeak that sounded like a mouse with the hiccups. Everyone was quite for a moment, and then someone started giggling. Soon the giggling erupted into full-fledged laughter.

"You call *that* a fart?"

"Does this mean we have to stay in school all summer?"

"He can't fart in front of us. Rudy Toot-Toot, how *prude*!"

Mr. Antwon felt bad for Rudy, and he knew there was only one way to help Rudy save face. He needed to divert the crowd's attention.

"School's out! Hurry or you'll miss your busses and you'll have to stay here until September," he said into the microphone.

The students cheered and ran to the line of busses waiting to take them home. Everyone except for Rudy.

"Rudy, hurry or you'll miss the bus," Mr. Antwon said.

"I don't care. If I ride the bus I'll just have to listen to everyone laugh at me more."

"It's not so bad. Remember when you got a detention because you were trying to make everyone laugh?"

"Yeah, but that's different."

"How so?"

"Because that time I was laughing, too. Now they're not laughing with me, they're laughing *at* me. I'd rather get in trouble for farting than not fart at all!"

They walked back to the school. Mr. Antwon called and talked to Mama and offered to drive Rudy home. After all, he explained, it was his idea to begin with.

"Don't worry, Rudy," Mr. Antwon said as they pulled into the Toot-Toots' driveway. "I'm sure your gas will be on again tomorrow. Have a good summer vacation!"

CHAPTER 7

By the Fourth of July all the beans were growing great. Even Mr. Anderson's corn looked better than it did last year. Big Bean Dean said it was because Rudy rotated the crops when he blew the soybeans into the cornfield. Papa seemed okay with that explanation and let Rudy help out more on the farm.

That summer was calm and relaxing and filled with good cheer. Every weekend they went to Mr. Anderson's dairy farm for ice cream. They even went into town and saw a movie and ate pizza at Emilio's twice.

Everything was back to normal.

Until the cicadas came.

~∞~

Rudy heard a weird buzzing noise coming from the big oak tree in the backyard. He climbed down from his fort atop the swing-set to investigate. As he got closer to the trunk of the tree, he noticed something crunching under his feet. He scanned the grass and saw tons of little bugs, each about an inch long.

The bugs weren't moving. He picked one up. It had legs and a head, but it also had a big hole in its back and it was empty inside.

A huge fly buzzed past him and landed on a leaf on a low branch. He looked up and saw dozens of the bugs chewing at the edges of the leaves. One flew down and landed on his arm. Rudy jumped and shook his arm but the bug didn't let go. It tickled where its legs gripped his skin, but it didn't bite him or sting him. Rudy ran to the barn to show Papa.

"Papa! You have to see this!" Rudy shouted as he burst through the doorway. Rudy held his arm out for his father to see, and he held up the dry little shell with his other hand.

"Oh, no!" Papa said. "This is not good. Dean, come over here," Papa called. He turned to Rudy. "Where did you find that?"

"In the back yard, they're all over the big tree," Rudy said.

Big Bean Dean hurried over to where Papa and Rudy were standing. "What is it...Oh, no! Cicadas!"

"What are cicadas?" Rudy asked.

"That bug on your arm is a cicada," Papa said.

"What about this little thing here?" Rudy asked, holding up the empty shell.

"That's a cicada, too," Big Bean Dean said.

"This..." Rudy asked, holding the tiny shell next to the huge fly-like cicada hanging from his forearm, "is the same bug as this?"

"Yes," Papa said. "The little shell is from a nymph. They live underground for seventeen years, then they crawl up out of the dirt and molt, shedding their skin like snakes. You see the hole in the top of the little shell you're holding? One of those big flies crawled out of that."

"Did you say seventeen years? That means this little bug is older than me!"

"Yes, and older than your sister, too."

"Are they dangerous?" Rudy asked.

"Extremely," Big Bean Dean said.

Rudy panicked. He ran around in circles flailing his arms and shouting for help. Papa grabbed him by the shoulders. "Calm down, cicadas aren't dangerous to you, but they will eat every single bean in our fields. Our entire crop could be ruined this year!"

CHAPTER 8

Papa called an emergency meeting in the warehouse. The whole Toot-Toot family and all the hired hands listened as Papa explained the situation.

"The cicadas are in the bean fields now. I can hear them out there. I called Mr. Anderson and he's got them in his cow pastures. All the other farmers in the area are finding them, too."

"What do we do to stop them?" Judy asked.

"Well, I hate to do this, but we're going to need to use chemical pesticides. I've hired a crop duster, but she's already booked until next Wednesday."

Rudy had never seen a crop duster before. He pictured a lady in a maid's outfit with a feather duster and a can of pesticide spray, dusting each plant the way he and Judy helped Mama dust the furniture in their house.

"So what do we do now?" Judy asked.

"Now we all need to walk the fields and survey the damage—and hope that next Wednesday won't be too late to save our beans," Papa said.

The whole crew took to the fields, walking carefully between the rows of beans and looking for cicadas. Rudy walked deep into the fields, his stomach rumbling. He needed a moment alone. Once he was a safe distance from everyone, he farted.

Pfft.

Most of the time Rudy's farts were really loud, but they weren't really stinky.

Pfft.

This time was not like most times.

Pfft.

It might have been the leftover baked beans he had for lunch.

Pfft.

Or maybe the bean-curd ice cream he ate that afternoon.

Pfft.

It could even have been the fried fava beans he ate for dinner the night before.

Pfft.

It was probably all of the above.

Pfft.

Hundreds of beans mixed together in his belly into a potent wind that was not only noisy, it was the most awful smelling gas Rudy had ever expelled.

Pfft.

The farts hung low to the ground like a fog, slowly drifting through the plants.

The gas hit a cicada, smacking it between its big eyes like a sucker-punch. The bug's wings twitched and its eyes watered. The fart surrounded the cicada so the bug had to hold its breath. The foul stench showed no signs of going away, and it wasn't the kind of bad smell you could just get used to after a while. It drove the bug from the plant and the cicada took to the air, gasping as it flew far from the Toot-Toot bean farm as fast as its wings would take it. It couldn't talk, but if it could it would have said, "Rudy Toot-Toot, how rude!"

Rudy walked through every row of every bean field, farting every step of the way.

The cicadas fled the fields behind him. They left all the Toot-Toot beans alone in favor of finding fresh air.

The Toot-Toots and the hired hands walked the fields every day after that—and never found another cicada.

When Wednesday rolled around, Rudy watched the road for the crop duster to drive by. He wanted to see what she looked like. To his surprise, she didn't wear a maid's outfit. Instead, she wore an aviator's jacket and goggles. And she didn't drive a car, she flew an airplane!

Papa and Big Bean Dean stood out in the middle of the fields and waved their arms back and forth in front of them, the way a football referee does when a field goal kick goes wide. The crop duster circled the field and flew off.

She came back flying low over the road. She landed and pulled up to the driveway.

"Am I too late?" she asked.

"Yes, but in a good way," Papa said. "The cicadas are gone, and they left the crops alone."

"How'd that happen?" the crop duster asked.

"Beats me," Papa said.

"I think I know," Big Bean Dean said. Everyone looked at him, eager to hear his explanation.

"Rudy already dusted the crops."

Now everyone looked at Rudy.

"Let me explain," Big Bean Dean said. Everyone looked at him again. "I was walking behind Rudy the day he first spotted the cicadas. I was downwind some of the time, so I know he was tootin' something wild that day. I didn't want to say anything about it, because that's not polite conversation. I noticed that cicadas flew away when he walked by, and I thought it was because Rudy spooked them. But what he really did was smoke them out with his farts! And it was so nasty they decided not to come back."

"You want a job, son? My name's Amelia," the crop duster said and shook Rudy's hand.

Rudy looked at Papa. "Can I?"

"Not this year," Papa said. "Amelia, Rudy's got an amazing gift, but he hasn't learned how to control it."

"How about a short ride in my plane instead? I have a few minutes to kill before my next job, since I'm not dusting your fields right now."

"Can I, Papa?" Rudy pleaded.

"Is it safe?" Papa asked Amelia.

"Sir, I wouldn't offer if it wasn't. I assure you he'll be safe as a bird while he's in the sky with me."

"All right then," Papa said.

Amelia climbed aboard, and Big Bean Dean lifted Rudy into the co-pilot's seat. Amelia helped Rudy fasten seatbelts across his lap and chest.

Rudy watched out the window as they took off, using the road as a runway. He waved goodbye to the ground as it fell away beneath him, the fields turning into patchwork as the plane climbed high into the air. The cornfield stuck out like a sore thumb among the bean fields, its tall, light crop in stark contrast with the darker, shorter beans.

"You like to go upside down?" Amelia asked.

"I don't know," Rudy said.

"Let's find out. You see that handle?"

Rudy nodded.

"Grab it and hold on, 'cause here we go!"

Rudy grabbed the handle and held on tight as the plane climbed straight up into the air. His seat tilted so far that he was lying flat on his back. The next thing he knew his knees were up higher than his chin and his seatbelt pressed against him as they went upside down. His feet came over his head and Rudy stared straight down at the ground. It felt like he was floating for a few seconds until the plane leveled out and he sank back into his seat.

"That was awesome!" Rudy said.

"I thought you would like it," Amelia said. "This is called a barrel roll."

The plane dipped down to the left and flipped over on its side and then came right-side up again.

"Whoa! This is better than a roller coaster!" Rudy laughed.

Amelia circled the farm and came in for a landing. Rudy thanked her, and Papa helped him climb down from the plane. They all waved to Amelia as she flew away.

After his stint in the air, Rudy was on cloud nine. But for all the glory he received for saving the farm from the cicadas, Rudy's real triumph was still a season away. His true day in the sun would come...after one long night.

CHAPTER 9

The first Saturday morning during the harvest was the opening day for the Bean Market. It was also the busiest day of the year on the Toot-Toot bean farm.

Rudy liked working at the family market. The days flew by because he worked so hard he never had a chance to look at the clock. It was the exact opposite of school, where there were clocks everywhere, constantly reminding Rudy that it was nowhere near time to go home.

Rudy also liked it when the market opened because that's when the Beanheads showed up. Every year, more and more Beanheads came to the Toot-Toot market. Rudy used to know them all by name, but he couldn't keep up anymore.

Rudy climbed out of bed and found a note on his bedside table. It read:

Rudy,

Good morning! We're short-staffed today, one of the hired hands is sick. I need you to help out. Here are five chores for you to do:

1. *Wake the Beanheads.*
2. *Go to the warehouse and take Inventory.*
3. *Update the Price Board.*
4. *Afternoon Bean Runner.*
5. *Ring the bell at Market Close.*

I know you'll do a great job. Mama and I will already be working when you read this, so you can just get started.

Thanks,

Papa

Rudy shook his head. He knew a lot about *growing* beans, but he didn't know anything about *selling* them. He wanted to ask Papa what he meant by words like "inventory" and "update" but Papa was already out working so Rudy couldn't ask him. His answer would probably take all day, anyway.

Rudy got dressed and went down to the kitchen. He knew he had a lot of hard work ahead of him, so Rudy ate a double-serving of Mama's famous 12-bean salad for breakfast. Then he went outside to do his chores. First on the list: *Wake up the Beanheads.*

The Beanheads camped out every night during the market season, eager to get to the counter early and buy the freshest beans. Their tents stretched down the road and over the hill as far as the eye could see. The multi-colored canopies looked like a never-ending rainbow, only instead of a pot of gold at the end there was a bag of beans.

Rudy walked down to the first tent. It was a black and red double-decker, one of the nicest tents in the line. It even had a doorbell. Inside slept twelve Beanheads.

Rudy reached out to ring the bell, but before his finger hit the button a fart burst forth from his bottom.

Pfffffffffffffffffffffffffffffffffffffffffffffffffffffft!

The tent flaps fluttered in its wind, sending a cascade of dew rolling off them like rain. "Abracadabra!" Rudy said with a smile.

All twelve people inside exclaimed in unison, "Rudy Toot-Toot! What a rude awakening!"

Rudy turned as red as a kidney bean and shuffled down to the next tent. This one was smaller, and it didn't have a doorbell. All Rudy needed to do was bend down and unzip the door so he could poke his head in and say good morning...without farting.

But as soon as he bent over another fart broke free, loud enough to echo off the hills and back down the row of tents over and over again, making one fart sound like a thousand.

"Abracadabra!" Rudy said again. But the only thing magic about the fart was that it woke up the rest of the Beanheads.

The echo of Rudy's fart faded, and taking its place arose hundreds of voices yelling, "Rudy Toot-Toot, how rude!"

At least the Beanheads were all awake. Rudy moved on to chore number 2: *Go to the warehouse and take inventory.*

CHAPTER 10

The beans were stored in a large warehouse that stretched more than half the length of the farm. The warehouse stood right next to the barn where they kept the tractors and other farm equipment.

The hired hands were already hard at work in the warehouse. One group sorted the beans and another group measured them out by weight then packed them into bags. They used 1-pound bags, 10-pound bags, and 100-hundred-pound bags for each kind of bean.

"I'm here to take inventory," Rudy said to a hired hand named Dave. "Can you tell me what that means?"

"Rudy, taking inventory means you count the beans," Dave explained.

Bean counting! Rudy liked to help out, but he hated math. To top it off, his belly still felt gassy and Rudy didn't want to be inside. The open air was always the best place to be when he had a biscuit in the oven, and Rudy was baking a Big One. He would much rather skip right to task three. But Papa had made his list of chores, and Rudy knew he had no choice but to complete them.

Rudy studied the warehouse. There were beans everywhere. They moved on long conveyer belts that looped around like giant snakes and twisted like pretzels. Some conveyor belts took the beans under hot-air Bean Blowers that dried them out to preserve them; other conveyor belts took the beans to cold rooms where they would stay fresh. In every corner of the warehouse, beans were piled up to the ceiling, and Rudy had to count them all!

"Good morning, Rudy. Here to do the counting?" asked Big Bean Dean.

"Yessir," Rudy said. He grabbed a clipboard and pencil and sulked his way over to the bags of beans.

"This is your first time taking inventory, isn't it?" Big Bean Dean asked.

Rudy nodded. "I have to count every bean. This is going to take forever!"

"It's not that bad. We count by how much the beans weigh, we don't count every bean. That would take forever!" Big Bean Dean winked at Rudy.

Rudy stared at the sea of bags covering the warehouse floor, grouped together by the color of the bag. The bags were set out in a big grid with rows and aisles criss-crossing between them. They looked like hills and cliffs, small bags gradually getting bigger, then falling off to another row of small bags and getting bigger again. Over and over. And then over and over again. There sure were a lot of bags. *This is going to take forever*!

Rudy's nerves made his stomach gurgle. He fought to hold the fart back. He had to concentrate so he could finish taking inventory as fast as possible.

"Why are there different colored bags?" Rudy asked.

"Each color represents a kind of bean. That way we know what kind of bean is in each bag," Big Bean Dean said.

"Why do you set them up this way?"

"It makes it easier to count the bags. Every row is ten bags wide."

Rudy scratched his head. "How does it make it easier to count when there are rows of ten?"

"I'll show you. How many one-pound red bags are there?"

Rudy pointed at each bag as he counted out loud. "One, two, three, four—"

Dean interrupted him. "Hold on, Rudy. You're doing it the hard way. Count the rows, but count by tens."

This time Rudy pointed at each row of small red bags as he counted out loud. "Ten, twenty, thirty, forty, fifty. There are fifty small red bags!" Rudy's tummy rumbled in excitement and the fart almost slipped out, but he stopped it at the last second. He had to hold it until he could get out of the warehouse.

"See how easy it is to count in tens? Now look at your clipboard and write *50* on the first line under *Red Bags*. But we're not done yet. We still have ten-pound bags and hundred-pound bags."

Rudy counted three rows of ten-pound bags and four rows of hundred-pound bags. He wrote *30* on the next line and *40* on the third line under *Red Bags.*

"Hold on, Rudy, not so fast. We're writing down the number of pounds, not just the number of bags," Big Bean Dean told him.

"Do I have to start all over? This pencil doesn't have an eraser," Rudy said. If he had to start all over there was no way he'd make it outside before he farted.

"Nope. This is super easy. You don't even need the eraser. I'll teach you how to multiply by ten and by one-hundred." Big Bean Dean told him.

Rudy groaned. The only thing he hated more than doing math was learning new things about it. There was always too much to remember. Besides, if he concentrated too hard on math problems, he was sure to lose control of the fart he was holding back.

"How many zeros are in a ten?" Big Bean Dean asked.

"One?" Rudy answered, thinking it was a trick question.

"Right. When you multiply by ten, you just take that zero and put it at the end of the number you are multiplying. So thirty times ten is?"

Rudy wrote a zero at the end of the thirty: *300*. "It's three-hundred. This is easy!" *Maybe I'll be able to hold it in after all…*

"I told you that using tens makes it easier to count! Multiplying by one-hundred is the same, you just take the zeros and add them to the end of the other number."

Rudy looked at the next line on the sheet. He had written down *40*. He wrote two more zeros: *4,000*. "There are four-thousand pounds of beans in the big red bags."

"Rudy, we'll make a bean counter out of you yet. One last step and we'll be ready to move on to the next color of bags. Now you need to add them up."

"No problem." Rudy wrote *4,350* on the last line under *Red Bags*.

Big Bean Dean patted him on the back. "Rudy, I think you can handle it from here. I need to go check on the load of beans coming in from the fields. Keep going, and come get me when you're done."

Rudy continued counting. He made great progress and relaxed a little bit as he added up the numbers for the last color of bean bags. But relaxing a little bit turned out to be relaxing too much. A loud grinding sound rose up to the rafters and bounced back down off the ceiling, reverberating into every corner of the huge warehouse.

"What is that noise?" asked one of the hired hands.

"Is the conveyor belt to the Bean Blower slipping again?" asked another.

"It sounds like the tractor's engine is about to explode!"

Something was about to explode alright, but it wasn't the tractor. Without further warning a mighty fart escaped from Rudy's backside.

Pfffffffffffffffffffffffffffffffffffffffffffffffffffft!

"Rudy Toot-Toot, how rude," the hired hands said in unison.

"Rudy, you're lucky we seal those beans in air-tight bags, otherwise you could have spoiled the entire crop. Nobody wants to eat a bean that tastes like a toot! Let me see how you did on the inventory," Big Bean Dean said, holding his nose.

Rudy handed him the clipboard and waited while Dean looked over the numbers. "This looks good," he told Rudy. "Now take it up to your Papa and you can start on your next chore." Big Bean Dean handed the clipboard back to Rudy.

"Sure thing. Thanks!" Rudy jumped at the chance to put the bean counting behind him and ran off toward the market. The hired hands jumped at the chance to let some fresh air in and opened all the doors and windows.

Rudy pulled Papa's note from his pocket. Next on the list: *Update the Price Board*.

CHAPTER 11

The Price Board was a great big chalkboard behind the cash register at the Bean Market counter. It listed all the prices for each size bag of each kind of bean. It was a vast sea of numbers and letters.

A long tray filled with chalk and erasers ran along the bottom of the board. Up at the very top, the board always said the month, day, and year. Rudy thought "update" meant to write a new, bigger date up on the board. That would be easy.

Rudy saw Papa standing behind the cash register.

"I have the inventory for you," Rudy said, handing his father the clipboard.

Papa looked at the inventory sheet. "This looks good. Great job, Rudy. Now I can calculate today's prices."

Rudy felt relieved that Papa was doing this part. He had done enough math for the day.

Papa pulled a laminated sheet of paper out from under the cash register. Rudy stared at it. It said *Price Sheet* at the top. It looked just like the Price Board, only much smaller.

Papa started hitting buttons on a calculator and a little sheet of paper started to emerge from its top. The paper grew and grew, coiling around like a snake. When Papa finished, he tore off the paper and looked at it as he wrote new numbers on the Price Sheet.

"How do you know what numbers to write?" Rudy asked.

Papa tried to explain, but Rudy didn't get it. *What does he mean by 'Supply and The Man'?* Rudy thought. *Why are prices higher when The Man is bigger?*

"How big does The Man have to be?" Rudy asked.

"What man?"

"Supply's man."

"There's no man. Supply is the beans."

"You said supply and The Man."

"Oh, no...I said supply and *demand*." Papa explained. He wrote the word across the bottom of the Price Sheet so Rudy could see how it was spelled. "Demand is how badly people want something. High demand means people really want it bad, low demand means not many people want it at all. Do you get it?"

"I think so," Rudy said. He still didn't get it, though.

Papa saw the puzzled look on Rudy's face. "Which do you like better, pizza or Brussels sprouts?" Papa asked.

"Pizza!" Rudy said.

"So for you, pizza is in higher demand because you want it more. I bet if you had one dollar to spend, and you had to choose between Brussels sprouts and pizza, you would pick pizza."

"Oh yeah!"

"Even if all you could get was one slice of pizza, but you could get one-hundred pounds of Brussels sprouts? It doesn't matter that you get more Brussels sprouts for that dollar?"

"No way! Pizza is better than a thousand pounds of Brussels sprouts. I'd pay ten dollars for a piece of pizza!"

"What if you had a hundred dollars? Would you spend that for one piece of pizza?"

Rudy thought about that. A hundred dollars was a lot of money. "Not for just one piece. I'd have to get a whole pizza for that."

"What if it was the last piece of pizza in the whole word?" Papa asked. "Would you pay one hundred dollars then?"

"Well..." Rudy thought it over. "I guess I would, if it was the last piece ever."

"That's supply and demand. A low supply and a high demand, like how much you would want the last piece of pizza on earth, means a higher price than a huge supply and a low demand, like the thousand pounds of Brussels sprouts that I can't even sell to you for one dollar."

"I get it now. That's cool!" Rudy said. He celebrated his newfound wisdom the best way he knew how: with a toot.

Pfft!

"Here's what you need to do next," Papa said as he wrote the final number on the Price Sheet and handed it to Rudy. "I need you to update all the prices on the board. Erase the old prices, and write in the new ones that are on the Price Sheet."

"So update doesn't just mean to write a bigger date up on the board?" Rudy asked.

Papa laughed. Adults always thought it was funny and laughed when Rudy asked smart questions like that.

"No, Rudy," Papa said. "Update means to make something current."

More big words! Rudy didn't know what *current* meant any more than he knew what *update* meant. But Papa wanted him to write in new numbers, so that's what he would do. Maybe *current* and *update* both meant *new*.

Rudy grabbed the eraser and climbed the stepladder so he could reach the first number. He erased the price for 1-pound bags of chili beans, then he climbed down to get a piece of chalk.

Papa stopped Rudy. "Let me give you some advice," he said. Papa gave everyone advice. "The easiest way to update the prices is to erase all the numbers first. Then get the chalk and write all the new prices on the board at the same time. That way you won't need to keep climbing up and down the ladder. It's more efficient."

What does 'efficient' mean? Rudy thought. *Maybe it's the same as 'easy.' Could Papa ever talk without using big words? Probably not. Mrs. Miller would be proud of him.*

Rudy put the Price Sheet down and as he reached for the eraser a gust of wind blew the Price Sheet to the ground. Rudy bent down to grab it and just when his butt was pointing up at the Price Board, he farted.

Pffffffffffffffffffffffffffffffffffffft.

"Abracadabra!" Rudy said.

"Rudy Toot-Toot, how rude!" Papa said. "The only thing magic about that fart was the disappearing trick."

"What disappearing trick?" Rudy asked, turning around. His fart blew the chalkboard clear! "Sweet! Now I don't have to erase all those numbers." Rudy ran and put the eraser back in the tray.

Papa held his chin in his hand. "Now that is efficient," he said.

Rudy finished updating the Price Board and Papa rang the bell to open the market. The Beanheads rushed to the counter in a frenzy.

Rudy climbed up to the fort atop his swing-set and watched the action. Hired hands picked beans in the fields, and tractors hauled the heavy loads back to the warehouse to be sorted and bagged so they could be counted and sold the next day.

The Beanheads waited in a long line. Once they bought their beans, they packed up their tents and headed home. But there sure were a lot of Beanheads. Hundreds of Beanheads who'd come to buy thousands of pounds of beans.

Chapter 12

Mama fixed lunch for Rudy and Judy: chili dogs. Of course the chili was made with Toot-Toot kidney beans and Toot-Toot chili beans, so it was the best around!

"Did Papa give you chores today?" Rudy asked Judy.

"Just one. I'm the Afternoon Bean Runner." Judy said.

Rudy pulled Papa's note out of his pocket. "But *I'm* the Afternoon Bean Runner!"

"No squabbling. There's going to be more than enough work for both of you," Mama said.

Bean Running turned out to be really fun at first. The Beanheads would tell Mama what they wanted, and Rudy and Judy fetched all the 1-pound and 10-pound bags for them while Papa rang them up at the cash register. The hired hands got the 100-pound bags.

The chili dogs had an odd effect on Rudy. Every time he stopped to rest they made him fart in bursts like a machine gun: *toot-toot-toot-toot-toot*. The farts only stopped when he started moving again.

Time flies when you're having fun. But when you're running away from toxic toots, it moves about as fast as a turtle running through peanut butter. Every minute lasted an eternity.

Rudy and Judy moved slower and slower as the afternoon wore on. They tried to keep up with the flood of orders pouring in, but they were exhausted. Even Mama, Papa, and Big Bean Dean slowed down. The Toot-Toot Bean Market had never seen a busier opening day.

The sun moved toward the horizon and Papa checked his watch and called to Rudy, "It's time for the Bean Market to close. Go ring the bell!"

Rudy remembered his list of chores. He pulled it from his pocket and read it while he ran. *Ring the bell at market close.*

"But there are still so many Beanheads waiting!" Rudy said, looking at the long line of people stretching all the way to the top of the hill and beyond.

"It's all right. Some Beanheads camp out several days waiting for their turn at the counter," Papa explained. "We can't stop taking orders until the bell rings. We can't do this all night. We have to stock up for the morning or we'll never make it through the day tomorrow!"

"Hurry, Rudy...before my arms and legs fall off!" Judy begged.

"Rudy, you need to ring that bell now!" Mama said.

Rudy ran to the bell. It looked like the Liberty Bell, only smaller and without the crack. A rope attached to a metal ringer dangled from inside the bell. Rudy thought the ringer looked like that thing that hangs down in the back of your throat.

Rudy reached out for the rope and gave a tremendous tug, but before the ringer hit the side of the bell it broke! The ringer fell down into the mud with a thud.

Now what? Rudy thought.

The noise from the market made it hard to hear Papa as he cupped his hands around his mouth and called for Rudy to ring the bell. Papa couldn't hear Rudy at all when he called back that the bell had broken.

The pressure mounted. The Beanheads knew the market was about to close, so they crammed toward the counter to try and place their last-minute orders. The noise grew louder as they called for sacks of their favorite beans. Now Rudy couldn't hear Papa at all.

Rudy had to do something, and he had to do it quick. Something...loud.

He ran to a little girl standing in line. He had never seen her before. She would be perfect. He asked her, and she did it.

She did what no Toot-Toot would do. Something that gave Judy nightmares. Every hired hand knew better than to do it. But she did not know better. So she pulled Rudy's finger.

It was just a little tug, but that's all it took. Like a hair trigger on a bazooka, the slight force of her hand on his unleashed an epic explosion:

PFFFFFFFFFFFFFFFFFFFFFFF

FFFFFFFFFFFFFFFFFFFFFFFF

FFFFFFFFFFFFFFFFFFFFFFFF

FFFFFFFFFFFFFFFFFFFFFFFF

FFFFFFFFFFFFFFFFFFFFFFFF

FFFFFFFFFFFFFFFFFFFFFFFF

FFFFFFFFFFFFFFFFFFFFFFFF

FFFFFFFFFFFFFFFFFFFFFFFF

FFFFFFFFFFFFFFFFFFFFFFFF

FFFFFFFFFFFFFFFFFFFFFFFF

FFFFFFFFFFFFFFFFFFFFFFFF

FFFFFFFFFFFFFFFFFFFFFFFF

FFFFFFFFFFFFFFFFFFFFFFFF

FFFFFFFFFFFFFFFFFFFFFFFF

FFFFFFFFFFFFFFFFFFFFFFFFT!

A loud clap like thunder rocked the entire farm. The monstrous emission actually lifted Rudy three feet into the air. The earth shook and all the people in line disappeared over the hill, running as fast as they could. The canopies of the Beanheads' tents were blown to shreds in the ensuing gust, and the tent poles cracked and collapsed upon the shaking ground.

The market was officially closed for the day. All of the customers were gone. The Toot-Toot family and the hired hands stood in stunned silence. Even the crickets stopped chirping.

"Well, that's one way to do it," Papa said. "Rudy, I think your timing was good, but you have got to control the power. I'm surprised nobody got hurt. A blast that big can be dangerous."

"Look at all the tents. They're ruined," Mama said. "Where will the Beanheads sleep tonight?"

"Not here, that's for sure," Judy said.

"Rudy, tomorrow you'll need to apologize to each Beanhead for destroying their tents and campsites," Papa said.

"Okay. I'm sorry, I was only trying to help," Rudy said. "The bell broke."

Rudy kicked a pebble and headed back up to the house to get cleaned up for dinner.

That night, after he ate, Rudy looked over Papa's shoulder as he wrote a new list of chores. This time they were his own. First thing on the list:

Fix that bell!

CHAPTER 13

The next day Papa repaired the bell in time for Market Open, but only the Toot-Toots and the hired hands heard it ring. There were no customers in sight.

"I bet it's because of Rudy's fart!" said Judy.

"Hush," said Mama.

They waited all day long but the Beanheads never came. Papa didn't even bother to ring the bell at Market Close.

"They'll be back tomorrow," said Papa. "They always come back."

The next day, the same thing happened…or didn't happen, depending on how you look at it. Not a single person stopped by. Not a single bean was sold. Not that week. Or the next week. Or the one after that.

Mama and Papa tried calling the Beanheads to get them to come back, but they refused. They were scared, and many didn't have enough money for beans because they had to replace all of their camping equipment.

Beans were piled up everywhere. The cold storage rooms were packed full. The rest of the inventory was starting to spoil. Big Bean Dean had to dry out extra beans under the hot air Bean Blowers to save them, but Papa knew that they were still losing a lot of money. Dry beans were never worth as much as fresh beans.

"I'm sorry, Papa," said Rudy as they looked over the warehouse, but Papa didn't notice. He just smoothed out a wrinkle on the pair of underwear he wore on the outside of his pants.

When school started back up, Rudy discovered that all the kids in his class knew about his blast. Instead of complimenting him on his quick thinking, or showing respect for his awesome power, they were afraid he would do it again. Nobody wanted to get their clothes blasted off, so none of the kids would sit next to him in class, and Rudy played alone at recess.

The Toot-Toots' problems got worse the next month when the bank called. Papa had to pay the bank each month for a loan. The problem was, without customers buying beans, his cash crop was a bust. The Toot-Toot family was flat broke, so Papa couldn't pay the bank.

The first thing the bank did was repossess their combine and a lot of the other farm equipment. The Toot-Toots had to pick the corn by hand, leaving the tall stalks to whither in the field. At least Mr. Anderson gave them milk and meat in exchange for the corn, so they didn't go hungry.

Next, the bank sent a letter telling Papa that if he couldn't pay, they would take the farm away. Papa had to lay off all of the hired hands just to keep the farm one more month while he tried to think of a solution. He even had to lay off Big Bean Dean (although Big Bean Dean promised to stay on with no pay). This was the biggest problem any of them had ever faced in their entire lives.

"How can the bank take our farm?" Judy asked. "Your great-great-grandfather owned this land, Papa. It's been in our family for years!"

"The bank gave us money last year. We needed it to expand the warehouse and upgrade all of our machinery. When a bank loans you money, you agree that if you can't pay them back, you will give them something else. In this case, it's our farm," Papa said.

"But why the farm? They took back the equipment we bought," Rudy said.

"That's not enough," Papa said. "The equipment has been used, so it's worth a lot less now than when we bought it."

"We need to find some way to get our customers to come back," Mama said.

"It's all Rudy's fault! Him and his stupid farts," Judy said.

Rudy couldn't take it. He ran up to his room and slammed the door. He tried not to cry, but he couldn't stop himself. He buried his face in his pillow so no one could hear him. He was just trying to help. Rudy thought he was doing something special when he farted and closed the market, but he had ruined everything. The Beanheads were all mad at him. The hired hands lost their jobs. His sister hated him. His parents were disappointed in him. And to top it all off, the bank was going to take away their home. All because of him. He wanted to run away, where nobody would know what trouble he was.

Mama knocked on his door. "Rudy?" she called softly.

Rudy didn't answer. He stopped crying and held his breath, trying to be as quiet as possible.

"Rudy, you sister was wrong to say that. She didn't mean it. Do you want to come down for dinner?" Mama asked through the door.

Rudy didn't answer.

"Okay. Come down when you're ready," Mama said. "We'll get through this. We always do."

Rudy curled up on his bed and hugged his knees against his chest. He stayed that way for a long time. He stayed that way as he listened to the clink of silverware on dinner plates, even though his tummy was rumbling (from hunger, not from gas). He stayed that way through the clatter of plates in the sink as Papa and Judy helped Mama do the dishes.

Rudy stayed that way until he heard a TV show echo up through the vents.

"Standing next to me is the owner of the fields where these mysterious markings appeared..." said the show's host.

Rudy kept listening, and an idea grew in his head.

CHAPTER 14

Downstairs, Papa was watching a documentary on UFOs. Rudy held his ear to the vent on his bedroom floor to hear better. The show's host described crop circles, spectacular patterns that mysteriously appeared in the middle of wheat and cornfields. Nobody knew who made them or why. While many thought that the crop circles were a hoax—a joke made by people to fool others—the narrator seemed to think UFOs could be making them, aliens flying over the fields at night and flattening the crops with strong winds made by their spaceships.

But regardless of who made them, wherever and whenever the crop circles appeared people came from miles around to see them. News helicopters flew overhead taking pictures that were broadcast on TV and printed in newspapers. The people who owned the fields became celebrities.

As Rudy listened, his idea grew more and more clear. He knew exactly what he would do. He wasn't sure if he could pull it off, but he had to try. After all, doing nothing sure wasn't going to solve the problem.

Several thoughts crossed his mind. *What if I get caught? What if it doesn't work? What if it just makes things worse?*

Rudy chased away his doubts and fears and concentrated on his plan. The time had come for Rudy to take charge. He had to set things right.

Rudy remembered what their cornfield looked like from the air. He got a piece of paper and a pencil from the desk in his bedroom and started to draw. He started at the top-left corner, and he drew a star. Below the star Rudy drew a crescent moon. In the center of the paper he drew the earth, and then surrounded it with a ring of beans. Up at the top-right corner he drew a curved line for the sun, so it looked like it was so big only a small part of it could fit on the paper.

Rudy held his drawing up and admired it. He folded the sheet and put it under his pillow. Then Rudy turned the light off, climbed into his bed, and pretended to sleep.

Mama came in to check on him after Judy went to bed. Rudy was awake, but he kept his eyes closed and fooled her. Mama kissed his forehead and left his room. Soon Rudy heard her and Papa go to bed. Then he climbed out of bed and got dressed.

Quiet as a mouse he crept from his bedroom and down the stairs. He stopped in the kitchen and grabbed a bowl of baked beans from the fridge. Rudy snuck out the back door. The nighttime air was chilly. There were no clouds. He looked up at the night sky. The light from the moon and all the stars seemed to beckon him on, urging him to go through with his plan. Rudy made his way to the edge of the cornfield—the starting line for all his troubles that year—and under the watchful eyes of the heavens he went to work. He needed to make things right for his family.

Rudy concentrated. He couldn't slip up this time. Papa said he needed to control his farts, and flattening corn to make crop circles would take massive control. Each fart had to be silent, so he wouldn't wake anybody up. Each fart had to be strong, in order to bend the stalks, but not too strong, or he would break them. And each fart had to land in exactly the right place, so the shapes would look right.

Rudy bent over and put his hands on his knees. He felt his tummy rumble. He closed his eyes and concentrated. In his mind's eye he saw his drawing, and he imagined his picture on top of the field behind him. The gas in his tummy swirled around until it had a sharp tip like a pencil. He pointed his butt up into the air and took aim. Rudy was in total control when he fired.

The fart sprang forth, straight up into the air, and its gas made a giant arc before coming down in the corner of the field. When it hit the ground it swirled like a tiny tornado, staying in one place and pressing the corn stalks into a small circle. Then the tornado collapsed to the ground and shot out in every direction. A pattern emerged in the top-left corner of the field: a little round star, with rays shining out all around it.

Rudy took a big bite of baked beans. He stood and stretched, letting his belly fill up with more gas. Once Rudy was sure the pressure inside him was just right he bent over again.

One, two, three...

With the corn as his canvas, Rudy farted with all the grace of a famous artist like Michelangelo adding a brush-stroke to his very best painting. This time the swirling point of his fart came down and drew the shape of a large crescent moon in the corn, right by his star.

It took three bites of beans to load up with enough gas to make the earth: A perfect circle in the exact center of the field. He had enough wind left in him to encircle the earth with beans and he fired off his farts faster, one after another, until the only thing left to draw was the sun.

Rudy downed the last bite of baked beans and got into position. He closed his eyes, imagining the bright warmth of the sun cresting the horizon to announce a new day—the day his family's problems would all be solved. Then Rudy did what he did best: he farted one more time.

Rudy's sun peered over the corner of the cornfield as the real sun splashed the eastern horizon with the lighter shades of day. Morning was upon him. Rudy hurried back toward the house before anyone woke up, stopping briefly to climb his swing-set and view his accomplishment from his fort. He could barely make it out from the low angle, but he could see it well enough. His crop circles had come out perfect.

Rudy went back inside, changed into his pajamas, and climbed into bed. He was asleep before his head hit the pillow.

CHAPTER 15

The sun rose over the Toot-Toot farm, its light reaching inside the windows of the house to wake up Mama, Papa, and Judy. It couldn't wake up Rudy, though. Lucky for him it was a Saturday and he didn't have to get up for school, so Mama let him sleep in.

When Rudy finally did wake up he went downstairs expecting everyone to be running around and talking excitedly about the crop circles in their cornfield. But they weren't. Mama and Papa were sitting at the kitchen table drinking coffee. Judy was reading a book. None of them had seen the field. Nobody knew about the clever designs waiting to be discovered in the corn.

Rudy wanted to tell Papa to go out and look, but he didn't want anyone to know that he made the crop circles. He waited and waited but Papa seemed inclined to stay inside all day long.

It was mid-afternoon when the phone rang. Mama answered it. She listened for a minute, and then handed Papa the phone and rushed to the window. Papa listened for a minute and then dropped the phone on the floor.

"That was the local TV station. A plane flying overhead saw something in our fields, like a crop circle. The pilot reported it to the airport, and they called the radio station. The DJ just mentioned it on the air. Now the TV station is sending a helicopter over to take pictures and a reporter to interview us!" Papa ran out the door before anyone else could speak.

Mama and Judy ran after him. Rudy got up slowly and walked out the door. As excited as he was that someone had spotted his design, Rudy worried that he might get into even bigger trouble if anyone found out it was a hoax. He had to play it cool.

Rudy joined his family in the yard. "Climb up here, you can see it better," Rudy beckoned from his fort atop the swing-set. He slid down the slide to make room as Papa, Mama, and Judy scrambled up the ladder.

For the first time in his life, Papa was speechless. After five minutes of staring at the field in silence, Papa finally found the right word to describe what he was seeing.

"Wow!" Papa said.

"Wow is right!" Mama agreed.

"How?" Judy asked.

"We may never know," Rudy said. *At least I hope not!*

They heard the *thump-thump-thump-thump* of helicopter blades off in the distance, getting louder every second. Papa slid down the slide and waved to the helicopter pilot, who circled the field once to get a good look and then landed in an open space in the yard. The pilot let the Toot-Toots sit in the helicopter so they could see the incredible crop circles from the sky.

Rudy looked down, impressed with his handiwork. He could draw better in corn with farts than he could on paper with a pencil or crayons!

"Are you getting this?" the pilot asked a cameraman who was also in the helicopter.

"You bet I am! This is the most amazing thing I've ever filmed," the cameraman answered.

Down on the ground, a news van raced along the road and pulled into the Toot-Toots' driveway. Its side door slid open and a pretty reporter got out holding a microphone. A man with a camera followed her. The helicopter came back down so the Toot-Toots could get out for an interview. The helicopter lifted back up into the air and the reporter started to speak into her microphone.

"I'm standing here live on the Toot-Toot bean farm where last night, something spectacular happened. Crop circles appeared in a cornfield. Are UFOs trying to tell us something? Astronomical markings are clearly evident: The sun, a star, the earth, and the moon. But there are also beans, a whole crop of beans circling the globe. Joining me now is Papa Toot-Toot. Tell me, do you know who made these amazing crop circles?"

"Nope," Papa said. He wasn't entirely lost for words, but they weren't coming easily. On top of his shock in finding crop circles in his field, he had terrible stage fright and the thought of being on live TV petrified him.

"Do you think these crop circles are extra-terrestrial in origin?"

"I...Uh...They...Um...Maybe."

The reporter could tell that the interview was falling flat. "Let's go back to our eye-in-the-sky and take another look at the incredible crop circles!" She lowered the microphone and thanked the family before climbing back into the van. The cameraman stowed his equipment and climbed into the driver's seat and they drove off.

Rudy watched them go down the road. As the van crested the hill, Rudy saw something glimmer in the afternoon sun, far off in the distance. It was the windshield of a car, heading toward the farm. There was another car behind it. And another. And another!

The road filled up with cars, vans, and trucks...all headed to the Toot-Toot farm.

Look at all of those people coming here! Rudy thought.

A long line of cars started pulling into the Bean Market parking lot. Passengers spilled out, gawked at the cornfield...and lined up at the market counter! All of the regular Beanheads showed up, along with many people the Toot-Toots had never seen before.

Big Bean Dean and the hired hands came, too. They were eager to see the crop circles first-hand. When they saw the line of people at the counter, they all knew that could wait. They had work to do.

CHAPTER 16

Rudy had never moved faster or worked harder in his entire life. He bet the same was true for everyone else on the farm. The Bean Market was swamped. People came from all over, and they kept coming, all through the night and into the next day. The Toot-Toots and the hired hands stayed up all night bagging and selling beans. Rudy worked so hard he didn't even notice how tired he was. Plus he was excited that his plan was so successful. Everyone who came to see the crop circles also bought some beans. The hired hands could barely fill the bags fast enough.

By the end of the next day, they were all out of beans. Every last one was sold. Papa's bumper crop turned into cash after all. The family did the only thing left to do: eat dinner and go to bed!

The following morning Rudy woke up and went downstairs. Mama and Judy were in the kitchen. "Where's Papa?" Rudy asked as he ate his breakfast.

"At the bank," Mama said. "But he wants to have a word with you when he gets home."

"About what?" Rudy asked. A nervous little toot slipped out. Getting a lecture was one thing, but *have a word with you* usually meant big trouble.

"I'm not sure. He didn't say."

Rudy went out to the swing-set and watched the road from his fort. When he saw Papa's truck coming down the road he walked over to the front porch and waited there. Papa parked and he and Big Bean Dean got out of the truck. Big Bean Dean headed out to the warehouse. Papa walked up to Rudy.

"I want you to come with me for a second," Papa said.

Rudy followed Papa out to the cornfield. *Uh-oh...*

"Do you remember going to bed last night?" Papa asked Rudy.

Come to think of it, Rudy didn't remember going to bed. "I guess not," he said.

"I didn't think so," Papa said. "You fell asleep at the dinner table and I carried you upstairs. You're getting really heavy!"

Rudy let out a nervous laugh.

"I found this under your pillow when I was tucking you in," Papa reached into his pocket and pulled out a folded piece of paper.

Rudy stopped laughing. *My drawing!*

"You did this, didn't you?" Papa asked, pointing at the cornfield.

There was no way out of this. Papa had caught him red-handed.

"Am I in trouble?" Rudy asked. "I was just trying to help."

Papa looked him in the eye. Rudy was sure he was going to get spanked and sent to his room for the rest of his life. His butt tingled in anticipation. But then Papa did something unexpected.

He smiled.

"You're not in trouble. Rudy, you saved the farm! We made more money yesterday than the last two years combined. The loan we took from the bank is paid back in full, and it's all because of your crop circles! I just want to know how you did it."

Rudy stood up straight and held his chin high. "I farted."

"Show me," Papa said.

Rudy bent over, hands on his knees, and he farted. The gas landed in a swirl and turned the crescent moon into a full moon, pushing down the stalks into a perfect circle.

"That's amazing," Papa whispered. "Rudy, I always knew you would find the right time and the right place to use your incredible gift. You have a lot of power at your fingertips. Well, maybe not at your fingertips, at your...let's just keep saying fingertips. It seems that you've finally learned how to use it."

"Want me to do more?" Rudy asked.

"Yes, but not right now," Papa said. "I need to go make a phone call."

CHAPTER 17

Papa had called the local news station. They sent the helicopter back out, along with three vans and a full team of reporters and cameramen. Papa also called the radio station, and they mentioned on-air that the Toot-Toots would reveal the secrets of their mysterious crop circles at five o'clock that evening. Cars flooded the Bean Market parking lot and the fields were packed with spectators expecting to see a UFO in the sky.

Rudy sat in the kitchen, huddled over his drawing. His pencil moved slowly, adding a final touch to the picture. He showed it to Papa.

"Yes, I think that's perfect," Papa said. Rudy showed it to Mama and Judy, and they nodded in agreement.

"I'm ready. Let's blow them away," Rudy said and winked.

The family walked out to the edge of the cornfield. Big Bean Dean and the hired hands had erected a platform and the news team set up a microphone and speakers. Huge TV monitors were also set up, showing a live video feed of the cornfield, shot by the cameraman in the helicopter. The Toot-Toots climbed the stairs to the top of the platform and looked out over the crowd. Rudy recognized many faces. He waved to Mr. Antwon and his classmates from school.

Papa stepped up to the microphone. His pride in his son outshined his stage fright, and he spoke with confidence. "Thank you all for coming out this afternoon. Two days ago, none of us could believe our eyes when we saw these amazing patterns in this cornfield. What's even more amazing is how they were made…"

"Was it a UFO?" someone called.

"That depends on how you define UFO," Papa said.

"How do you define it?"

"Would you like a definition, or a demonstration?"

Papa's reputation as a long-winded talker was well known around town, and no one wanted to wait around to listen to his definition, which would probably take several hours. The crowd agreed on a demonstration.

"Okay then, we'll show you. Feast your eyes on this!" Papa said.

The crowd looked to the sky, expecting an alien spaceship, but all they saw was the news helicopter. Then they heard a whoosh of wind and the rustling of corn stalks. The crowd turned their attention to the TV monitors and gasped when they saw the letter *T* appear in the cornfield. It was quickly followed by an *h* and an *e*.

"I don't believe it! Rudy Toot-Toot is doing it!" Mr. Antwon shouted, pointing at Rudy.

"Abracadabra!" Rudy said into the microphone.

"That's right," Papa said. "Our UFO isn't an Unidentified Flying Object. It's an Unbelievable Farting Object!"

Someone in the crowd yelled, "Do it again!"

Rudy concentrated and let loose another burst. More letters appeared in the field. Rudy kept farting and the crowd watched as the letters formed words, and the words formed a sentence:

The best tootin' beans this side of the moon!

The crowd broke into a thunderous applause. Papa hoisted Rudy up onto his shoulders. Mama and Judy stood next to them and cheered.

Rudy looked out over the faces in the crowd. People smiled and clapped their hands. The air filled with whistles and woots, all directed at one little boy and his spectacular fart-art.

After all his ups and downs, after hours in detention and days spent grounded from helping on the farm, Rudy had found his comfort zone. There on the stage, in front of hundreds of fans and a chorus of applause, he felt at home.

I wish this could last forever! Rudy thought and he held up his hand with his index finger outstretched in an *I'm number one!* gesture. Or perhaps it was a *Pull my finger!* gesture. Either would have been appropriate.

The next day, Rudy was the talk of the town. Everyone at school congratulated him and gave him high-fives, even old Mrs. Miller. The news station ran the footage over and over, and people called in to the radio station to tell the DJ what it was like watching Rudy in person. The mayor even gave him a key to the city. But all of that paled in comparison to the real grand prize: Free pizza for life at Emilio's. They even agreed to make special deliveries out to the farm!

Later that night, Rudy took a bath and got ready for bed. He put his hands behind his head and laid back onto his pillow. Mama opened the door and walked to the edge of his bed. She sat down beside him and tousled his shaggy red hair.

"I'm really proud of you," she said and kissed Rudy's forehead. "Papa and Judy are proud, too. And so is the rest of the town, for that matter. Who knew that farting could be such a magical talent? It's in the way that you use it, though. Like Papa always says, there's a time and a place for everything. Learning where and when is just part of growing up." She got up and walked to the light switch.

"Mama?" Rudy asked.

"Yes, Rudy?"

"I want to do it again. It felt good when people clapped and cheered and called for more. Nobody said 'Rudy Toot-Toot, how rude!'"

"I'm sure you'll have your chance, and one day the rest of the world will get to know Rudy Toot-Toot, too."

Mama turned off the light and closed the door. Rudy closed his eyes.

I did it, he thought. *Today the bean farm, tomorrow the world...* The smile still lingered on his lips as he drifted off to sleep.

About the Author

Rick Daley lives in Lewis Center, OH which can be really awesome except the weather is bad a lot.

He has a wife and two sons, and they all live with a neurotic schnauzer named Leo.

Rick is also the author of *The Man in the Cinder Clouds,* a gripping tale about Kris Kringle and how he came to be known as Santa Claus. It wasn't easy.

Rick's hobbies include cooking, playing guitar and bass, running, yoga, and wrestling great white sharks.

Just kidding about that last one.

Acknowledgements

This all started when my older son was about three years old. He tooted one day and I said, "Who are you, Rudy Toot-Toot?"

He asked, "Who's that?" Good question. I wasn't too sure so I had to make something up on the spot.

"He's a little boy who was born on a bean farm," I said. And thus the story began...

~∞~

Many years have passed and many things have happened since that fartful...er, fateful day. I came to this point with the assistance, guidance, and friendship of a multitude of people, some of whom I will probably forget to name here:

Angie, Max, and Vic for always being there; Brenda Bowen for helping me find a voice for Rudy's story; Sue Quinn, Laurel Montgomery Spatz, Joshua McCune, Donna and Clay Hole, and Sheryl Hart for your editorial feedback; Roy and Rosie Daley; Tyler and Anika Clark; the whole darn Ashkettle family, even the dogs; Ethan Borkowski and Andrew Wander for the first Rudy fan-fiction, and the rest of the students at Freedom Trail Elementary School for laughing so loud; Tracy McKenzie, Angela Moore, Steve Sargent, and the rest of the teachers and administrators at Freedom Trail; and, saving the best for last, thanks to my parents for helping to make me who I am.

Made in the USA
Monee, IL
09 December 2024